Marley and the Magical Candy Cane

By Ana Maria Medici

Illustrated by Michael McCabe

Edited by Brooke Vitale

Marley grinned as she looked around at
San Francisco's Union Square. From her place
in line to meet Santa, she could see an ice
skating rink and hear Christmas carolers.

In the middle of the square sat a grand Christmas tree, its strings of twinkling lights glowing on all the childrens' faces. Marley loved Christmas. It turned everything, no matter how ordinary, into a winter wonderland.

As the line moved up, Marley noticed a sign:

Seeing the words, a stream of tears rolled down Marley's face. She wanted so badly to meet Santa, but she knew her family didn't have the money.

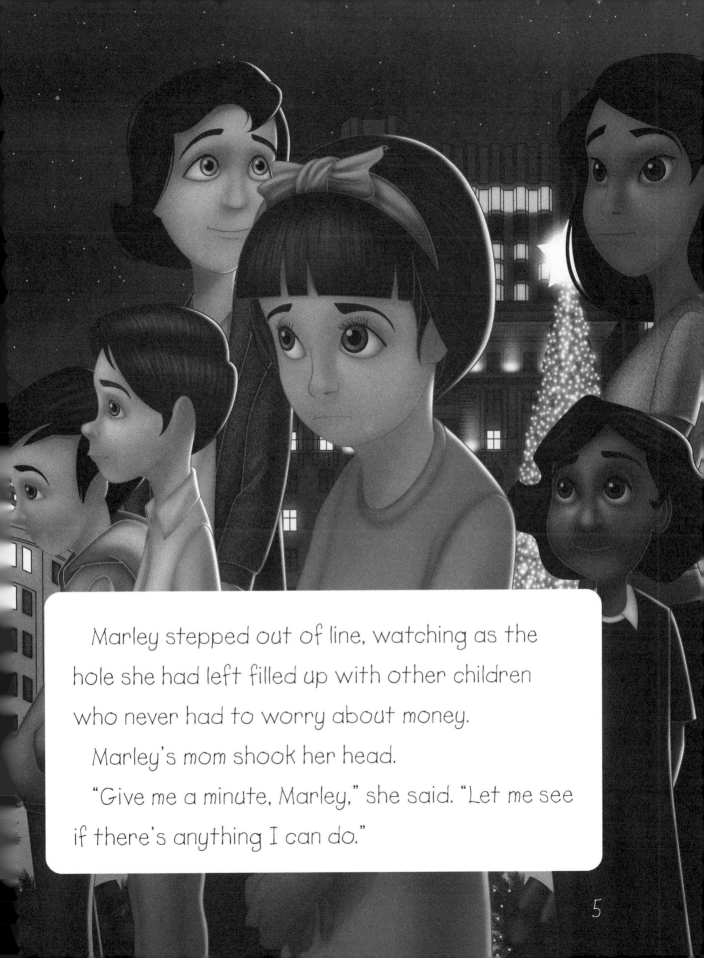

Marley stepped out of line, watching as the hole she had left filled up with other children who never had to worry about money.

Marley's mom shook her head.

"Give me a minute, Marley," she said. "Let me see if there's anything I can do."

5

Marley's *mom* walked over to the person in charge and tapped him on the shoulder.

"Excuse me, sir," she said. "I realize you're busy, and I'm so sorry to bother you. My daughter just wants to meet Santa, but we can't afford the ticket."

Reaching around her neck, Marley's mother took off her necklace. "Perhaps I could pay with this necklace? We don't need a picture, and we're happy to wait last in line. Please. It's Christmas."

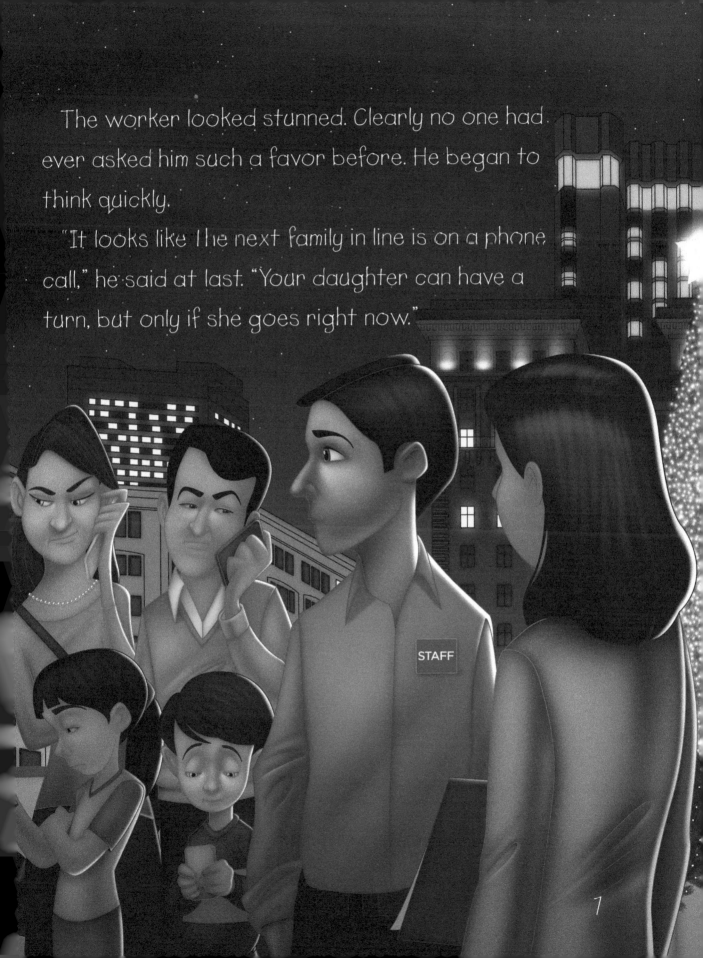

The worker looked stunned. Clearly no one had ever asked him such a favor before. He began to think quickly.

"It looks like the next family in line is on a phone call," he said at last. "Your daughter can have a turn, but only if she goes right now."

7

Seeing her mother wave her over, Marley ran as fast as she could to sit with Santa.

"Tell me Marley, what would you like for Christmas this year?" Santa asked.

Before she could answer, Marley's stomach growled. Usually her family ate dinner at the San Francisco Soup Kitchen—a place that served free meals to those in need. But tonight they had skipped dinner so that she could see Santa.

Marley hesitated, embarrassed by the noises coming from her stomach, and afraid to ask for help. What she needed this year wasn't a toy or a bike or anything else the other kids in line may have asked for. Marley was looking for a miracle.

"I need food Santa," Marley said finally. "My stomach growls at night, and sometimes I have a hard time falling asleep. My mom and dad try to share their food with me so I won't be so hungry, but they need to eat too." Marley hadn't realized it, but halfway through her request she had burst into tears.

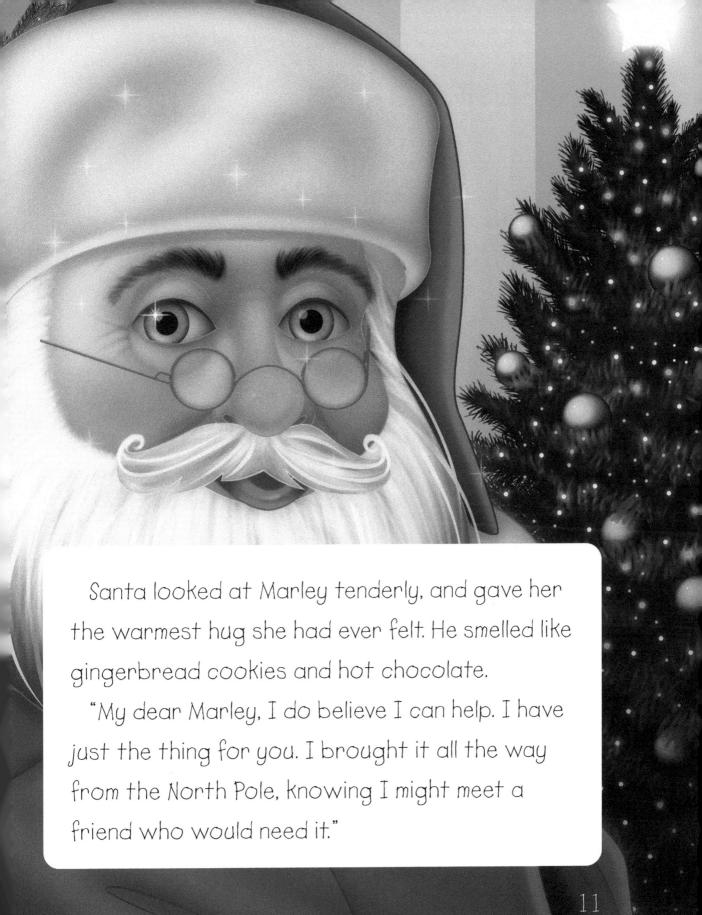

Santa looked at Marley tenderly, and gave her the warmest hug she had ever felt. He smelled like gingerbread cookies and hot chocolate.

"My dear Marley, I do believe I can help. I have just the thing for you. I brought it all the way from the North Pole, knowing I might meet a friend who would need it."

11

Marley watched as Santa reached into his bag, eager to see what he had, but all he brought out was a regular looking candy cane.

"Now, now," Santa said, as if reading her mind. "This is no ordinary candy cane. This is a *magical* candy cane. Tonight when you're tucked in bed and your stomach begins to rumble, take a small bite. I think you'll be surprised."

"Oh, thank you Santa!" Marley exclaimed, jumping down excitedly.

She had never had anything from the North Pole before.

That night as Marley was dozing off, she felt her stomach rumble. Unwrapping the tip of the candy cane, she took a small lick. Suddenly, Marley's mouth filled with the flavors of all her favorite foods: mashed potatoes, smoked ham, and peas in gravy. Even more amazing, Marley's stomach felt full!

The next morning, Marley raced to her parents' room. "Mom, Dad! Think of your favorite breakfast! Now have a taste of this candy cane." Marley's parents were confused, but they did as she asked. A moment later, a look of amazement came over their faces.

In school later, Marley fidgeted in her seat. It was the last day of school before Christmas break, and her classmates were happily dropping off Christmas gifts for their teacher, Ms. Fantastic. Marley hadn't eaten any lunch. She was eager to get home and take another taste of her candy cane, but she didn't want the other students to see her gift.

As soon as everyone had left, Marley gently set her painting down between the costly gifts. She knew it wasn't as nice as the presents the other kids had bought, but she had worked on it every day for a week, pouring all her love for her teacher into it.

Dear Ms. Fantastic,
Thank you for always reminding me to be kind.
Merry Christmas.
Love, Marley

At the sight of the painting, Ms. Fantastic's face lit up.

"Marley, I can see that you worked very hard on this, but I'm most pleased that you followed through with your giving."

"Followed through with my giving?" Marley asked.

Ms. Fantastic nodded. "Sometimes we get an idea to give, but we stop ourselves, for lots of different reasons. It's important that we follow through with what our heart first told us. We can all be kind and generous, in our own way. A gift doesn't need to be expensive, as long as it's from the heart. Thank you Marley."

Marley smiled back at Ms. Fantastic. She had just come up with a wonderful idea.

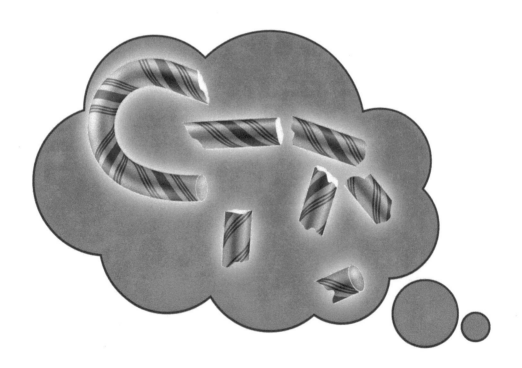

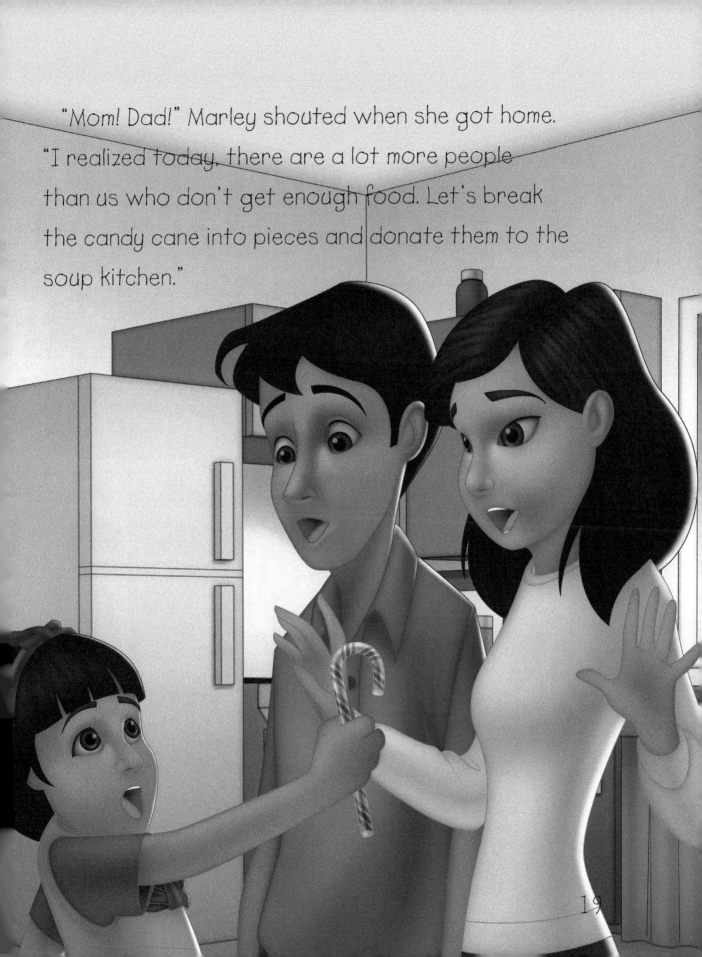

"Mom! Dad!" Marley shouted when she got home. "I realized today, there are a lot more people than us who don't get enough food. Let's break the candy cane into pieces and donate them to the soup kitchen."

19

That evening, the San Francisco Soup Kitchen opened early for their Christmas dinner. Marley and her parents arrived just as the doors opened, each holding a bag full of magic.

One by one, Marley handed out pieces of the
candy cane to the people eating at the soup
kitchen. Standing by the door, she smiled at the looks
of disbelief and joy surrounding her as everyone
discovered the magic of the candy cane.

Marley was just sitting down to eat her own dinner when a mother with two children approached her.

"Thank you," the mother said. "Tonight, for the first time in weeks, my children truly feel full. You are our own Christmas miracle."

Marley grinned, happy to see that, in her own small way, she had been able to make a difference.

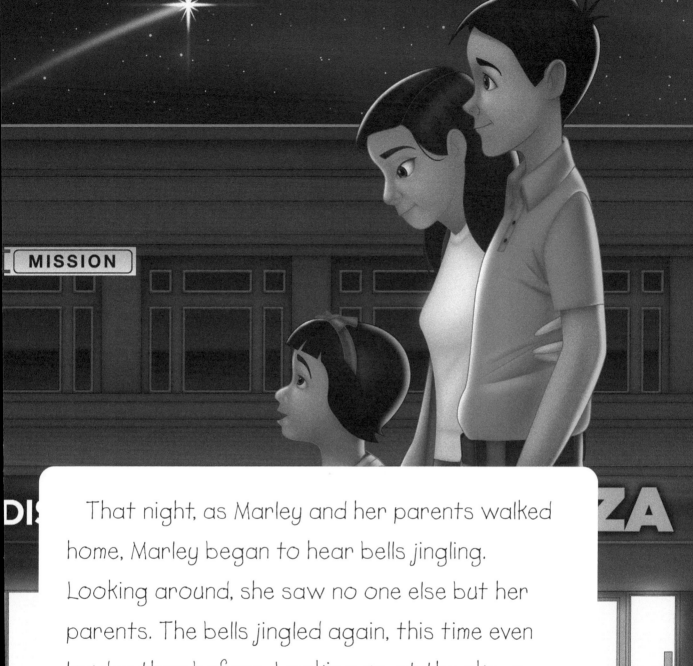

MISSION

That night, as Marley and her parents walked home, Marley began to hear bells jingling. Looking around, she saw no one else but her parents. The bells jingled again, this time even louder than before. Looking up at the sky, a twinkling flash of light streaked across the sky. Marley grinned, "Thank you Santa," she whispered. "Thank you, and Merry Christmas."

And there are those who
have little and give it all.
These are the believers in life
and the bounty of life,
and their coffer is never empty.
There are those who
give with joy,
and that joy
is their reward.
-Khalil Gibran

Dedicated to Larkin and Pender;
for helping me discover the story of Marley.

A special thank you to Beehive Illustration,
Michael McCabe and Brooke Vitale.

CPSIA information can be obtained
at www.ICGtesting.com
Printed in the USA
BVHW020715240920
589519BV00003B/19